# JALEN'S BIG CITY LIFE

# BAKING BUDDIES

by **Dorothy H Price** illustrated by **Shiane Salabie**

raintree 🍃

a Capstone company — publishers for children

Raintree is an imprint of Capstone Global Library Limited,
a company incorporated in England and Wales having its
registered office at 264 Banbury Road, Oxford, OX2 7DY –
Registered company number: 6695582

Edited by Alison Deering
Designed by Jaime Willems
Production by Whitney Schaefer

Design element: Shutterstock: Alexzel, Betelejze,
cuppuccino, wormig


978 1 3982 5312 4

**British Library Cataloguing in Publication Data**
A full catalogue record for this book is available from
the British Library.

Printed and bound in India.

# CONTENTS

# MEET JC

Hi! My name is Jalen Corey Pierce, but everyone calls me JC. I am seven years old.

I live with Mum, Dad and my baby sister, Maya. Nana and Pop-Pop live in our block of flats too. So do my two best friends, Amir and Vicky.

My family and I used to live in a small town. Now I live in a big city with tall buildings and lots of people. Come along with me on all my new adventures!

# Chapter 1

# SOMETHING SWEET

JC and Maya were spending

the day with Pop-Pop. When

they got home from the park,

JC's stomach grumbled.

"Sounds like someone's

hungry," Pop-Pop said.

"Ready for lunch?"

"Yes, please!" said JC.

"What about you, Maya?"
Pop-Pop asked. He tickled
Maya and made her giggle.

Pop-Pop led the way to the
kitchen. He pulled out all the
ingredients to make a sandwich.

JC sat at the counter to eat.

Pop-Pop put Maya in her high

chair. He fed her baby food.

"That was a good sandwich,

Pop-Pop," JC said.

Pop-Pop bowed. "I'm glad

you liked it."

"How about a sweet treat next?" JC suggested. "I could make some cupcakes."

"That sounds like a sweet idea," Pop-Pop agreed. "Let's find a good recipe."

Pop-Pop found a cookbook.
Then he and JC got out the
ingredients. They had everything
they needed to make cupcakes!

# Chapter 2

# BEING PATIENT

Before JC and Pop-Pop could start baking, they had to look after Maya. She usually had a nap after lunch.

Pop-Pop put Maya in her cot for her nap. But Maya was not sleepy. Every time Pop-Pop left the room, she cried.

Maya stood up and threw her dummy on the floor. JC washed it and gave it back to her. Maya threw it on the floor again.

Nothing seemed to work.
Maya being awake was very
distracting. It made it hard to
focus on the cupcake recipe.

Pop-Pop tried holding Maya.
He rocked her in his arms.

JC was frustrated. "We
can't bake cupcakes if Maya
is awake," he complained.

"Give her some time. She'll be sleepy soon," Pop-Pop replied.

Pop-Pop walked around the flat with Maya in his arms. He tried laying her down again. Maya's head popped back up.

"It's not working," JC said.
"Why isn't she sleepy?"

"She's just a baby," Pop-Pop
said. "We have to be patient."

JC frowned. He really wanted
cupcakes. His little sister was
getting in the way. How could
he and Pop-Pop bake if Maya
wouldn't fall asleep?

# Chapter 3

# NAP TIME

JC went back to the kitchen.

He stared at the cupcake recipe.

They needed flour, sugar, baking

powder and salt. They also

needed eggs, butter and milk.

*That's it!* JC realized. He ran

back to the other room.

"Pop-Pop!" he exclaimed.

"Maya needs her milk to fall

asleep."

Pop-Pop shook his head.
"How did I forget that?"

JC grabbed Maya's bottle from
the fridge.

"I'll get the warm water,"
he said. "Maya doesn't like
cold milk."

Pop-Pop smiled. "You're a great big brother, JC"

JC filled a bowl with warm water. He put the bottle in it.

"I guess this is Maya's treat," JC said.

"Yes, it is," Pop-Pop agreed.

Pop-Pop gave Maya her
bottle. He rocked her in his
arms. He walked with her
around the flat. Then he laid
her down in her cot. Maya
was fast asleep.

"Ready to make cupcakes?"
Pop-Pop asked.

"Yes!" JC cheered. Being
patient had paid off.

# Chapter 4

# A SWEET SNACK

JC and Pop-Pop got busy

baking. JC helped measure

the ingredients. They mixed

everything together in a big

bowl. Then they poured the

batter into a cupcake tray.

"These are going to be so yummy," JC said.

Pop-Pop put the cupcakes in the oven. JC set the timer.

Then they heard a noise from the other room.

"Uh-oh," JC said. "I think Maya is awake."

Pop-Pop grinned. "She must smell our cupcakes," he said. He got Maya from her cot.

Soon, the timer buzzed. Pop-Pop took the cupcakes out of the oven. While they cooled, JC played with Maya. Then it was time to ice them.

"Let's eat," Pop-Pop said when they had finished.

JC took a big bite. "*Mmmmm! They're delicious!*" he said. "This is the best."

"Do you know why?" asked Pop-Pop.

"Why?" JC answered.

Pop-Pop smiled. "Because

they were baked with love."

# GLOSSARY

**batter** mixture made of flour, butter, sugar and eggs that is used to make cakes

**distract** draw attention away from something

**focus** keep all your attention on something

**ingredients** different things that go into a mixture

**patient** staying calm during frustrating or difficult times

**recipe** directions for making and cooking food

# A SWEET TREAT

JC wanted to make cupcakes as his sweet treat, so Pop-Pop found the perfect recipe. What would you suggest making if you were wanting something sweet? Find a recipe in a cookbook or ask a parent or carer to help you find one online. Then have fun baking a sweet treat, just like JC!

# LET'S TALK

1. Pop-Pop tells JC he is a good big brother. What do you think makes a good big brother or sister? Do you think there are any hard parts about being the older one?

2. Cupcakes come in many flavours. What's your favourite? If you could create your own cupcake flavour, what would it be? What icing or toppings would you include?

3. What else could JC have done to keep Maya busy while he and Pop-Pop baked? Talk about some other ideas.

# LET'S WRITE

1. JC and Maya spent the day hanging out with Pop-Pop. Have you ever spent the day with a grandparent or other family member? What did you do for fun? Write a list of your activities.

2. Where do you think the rest of JC's family was during this story? Imagine you are JC. Write a letter to Mum, Dad or Nana telling them about your day.

3. Pop-Pop tells JC that their cupcakes were extra delicious because they were baked with love. Draw a picture of some other delicious foods that are baked with love.

# ABOUT THE CREATORS

**Dorothy H Price** loves writing stories for young readers. Her first picture book, *Nana's Favorite Things*, is proof of that. Dorothy was a 2019 winner of the We Need Diverse Books Mentorship Program in the United States. She hopes all young readers know they can grow up to write stories too.

**Shiane Salabie** is a Jamaica-born illustrator based in Philadelphia, USA. When she moved to the United States, she discovered her first true love: the library. Shiane later realized that she wanted to bring stories to life and uses her art to do so.